HEARTLINES

Heartlines

A Love Story

A Play by

Sarah Gabriella Waisvisz

Talonbooks

Talonbooks
9259 Shaughnessy Street, Vancouver, British Columbia, Canada V6P 6R4
talonbooks.com

Talonbooks is located on xʷməθkʷəy̓əm, Sḵwx̱wú7mesh, and səlilwətaɬ Lands.

First printing: 2025

Typeset in Minion 3
Printed and bound in Canada on 100% post-consumer recycled paper

Cover by Claude Cahun (1894–1954), *Self portrait (reflected in mirror)*, 1928, and Claude Cahun (1894–1954), *Suzanne Malherbe / Marcel Moore looking into mirror*, 1928, both courtesy of the Jersey Heritage Collections

Talonbooks acknowledges the financial support of the Canada Council for the Arts, the Government of Canada through the Canada Book Fund, and the Province of British Columbia through the British Columbia Arts Council and the Book Publishing Tax Credit.

Library and Archives Canada Cataloguing in Publication

Title: Heartlines : a love story / a play by Sarah Gabriella Waisvisz.
Names: Waisvisz, Sarah Gabriella, author.
Description: In English, with scattered text in French or German.
Identifiers: Canadiana 20250199955 | ISBN 9781772016970 (softcover)
Subjects: LCGFT: Historical drama. | LCGFT: Drama.
Classification: LCC PS8645.A4528 H43 2025 | DDC C812/.6—dc23

This play is dedicated to the heroes in my own family – Madeleine Desché, Bernard Huët, David Shentow, Jacques Maurits Waisvisz, Pierre Hardy Zizine – as well as to those fighting tyranny everywhere.

For Camille Rudney, who led me to these artists.

Je suis l'un, tu es l'autre. Ou le contraire.
Nos désirs se rencontrent.

—CLAUDE CAHUN

Aveux non avenus (1930)

A poem ... can be a message in a bottle, sent out in the – not always greatly hopeful – belief that somewhere and sometime it could wash up on land, on heartland perhaps.

—PAUL CELAN

"Speech on the Occasion of Receiving the Literature Prize of the Free Hanseatic City of Bremen" (1958)

PLAYWRIGHT'S PREFACE

How did I come to this story, or how did this story come to me? There are two inciting incidents.

The first happens in New York City, circa 2007, during one of my several visits to see Camille. One day a week, the Museum of Modern Art (MoMA) offers free entrance if you line up outside for hours. We do this. I have never been to MoMA, and we wander all around. At MoMA that day Camille and I take in a film screening: without any preconceived ideas, we watch *Lover Other*, the 2006 documentary film by Barbara Hammer about Lucy Schwob, a.k.a. Claude Cahun, and Suzanne Malherbe, a.k.a. Marcel Moore. It is a strange film with odd music, nonnaturalist acting, and a story we had never heard: the love affair between two French artists, stepsisters through their parents' marriage, who also managed to take up acts of resistance in WW II even though one was of Jewish heritage. We are mesmerized by the film. How could this story possibly be true? We too are French, Jewish, queer activists and would-be artists. We need to know more.

Circa 2016, two playwright friends and I start a "Queer Playwrights Unit" in Ottawa. We wish there were more queer plays, so we sit around lamenting this. We mostly drink tea or gin and tonic, and we talk about the writing we wish we were doing. One day we dare ourselves to *actually write something*. We know that we need a dose of the exquisite pressure of an opening night, so we book a venue at a local theatre and begin to promote an event, a "Queer Theatrical Salon" that would feature three new short plays, yet unwritten, that we would "lightly stage" and produce. I begin to write *Heartlines* as a response to this "dare," and what emerges is twenty minutes of early material, including the bones of several scenes that still appear in the script today. In this early staged reading, I play Suzanne, and Margo MacDonald plays Claude. We reprise this event at Toronto Pride that year and the feedback is so electric, I keep writing.

The more I explored the world of Lucy Schwob and Suzanne Malherbe, the more I saw how many holes and inconsistencies there were in the research, as well as how significantly the critical reception of the artists and their work had shifted over time. These inconsistencies were fruitful for me as a playwright, because I could insert my own ideas and interventions into or alongside what seemed like murky elements in the historical record. Some big questions became open for interpretation as a result, including questions about religion and gender. For example, is Suzanne Malherbe Jewish too? Malherbe is buried beside her beloved in the cemetery of St. Brelade's Church, Jersey, next to their old house. The gravestone is inscribed with not one but two Stars of David. Additionally, Malherbe grew up speaking German at home, which many German Jews who immigrated to France also did, but historical records list her as Catholic. In my play, I write Suzanne as a "fellow traveller," someone who is practising Judaism because she feels called to it.

Another key question concerns the gender identity of Claude Cahun. In *Disavowals* (1930), they write, "Masculine? Feminine? It depends on the situation. Neuter is the only gender that always suits me."* Yet we don't know exactly how Schwob would identify in today's gender terms. Despite their lifelong obsession with exploring gender, in their writing they used feminine adjectives to describe themself; however, it must be underlined that this writing was done in a historic French context. L'Academie française is only now beginning to relax its linguistic rules about gender in language and grammar. Consequently, I honour Schwob by using their androgynous chosen artist's name, Claude, throughout the script, and I try to capture their gender nonconformity in a nuanced way. I truly hope that Suzanne and Claude would approve of both of my bold choices.

* Claude Cahun, *Disavowals: or Cancelled Confessions* (originally published in French as *Aveux non avenus* by Éditions du Carrefour, 1930), translated by Susan de Muth (MIT Press, 2008), 151.

PRODUCTION HISTORY

Heartlines had its professional mainstage premiere at Great Canadian Theatre Company (GCTC) in Ottawa, Ontario, from March 22 to April 2, 2022, produced by Calalou/RAFT Theatre Projects in collaboration with GCTC and TACTICS, with the following cast and crew:

CLAUDE	Margo MacDonald
SUZANNE	Maryse Fernandes
BANDLEADER	Scottie Irving

Director and Dramaturge	Rebecca Benson
Sound Designer/Music	Scottie Irving
Video Designer	Kim Kölle Valentine
Lighting Designer	Tristan-Olivier Breiding
Costume Designer	Vanessa Imeson
Set and Props Designer	Andrea Steinwand
Intimacy Coach	Megan Piercey Monafu
Video Mapping Technician	Andrew Galligan
Production Manager	Christine Hecker
Stage Manager	Rebecca Eamon Campbell
Assistant Stage Managers	Arielle Voght and Yutong Ngui Wei

Heartlines underwent two development workshops supported by TACTICS and the undercurrents festival. During its writing, the playwright was in residence at GCTC and then the National Arts Centre. The play had its festival premiere at the undercurrents festival in 2020.

CHARACTERS

CLAUDE	Claude Cahun, born Lucy Schwob, an artist
SUZANNE	Suzanne Malherbe, a.k.a. Marcel Moore, an artist
BANDLEADER	A musician and witness

SETTING

The realm of memory

PRODUCTION NOTES

Each "Ode" in the play is a clown scene (interlude or lazzi): highly theatrical, ironic, absurd, and different from what comes before and after.

All radio broadcasts can be spoken live or prerecorded by the Bandleader.

A double slash // indicates lines spoken at the same time.

PLAYWRIGHT'S NOTE

The play is written in English, but in the world of the play, the characters are speaking French. They also speak German, Hebrew, and Yiddish. In Act 2 I have tried to reflect the bilingual linguistic environment of the island of Jersey. For both the first festival production at undercurrents (2020) and the premiere at Great Canadian Theatre Company (2022), design choices were made by the artistic team that reflected many years of collaborating on the world of the play. In the production at GCTC, we also included an original video design created by Kim Kölle Valentine that enhanced the stage presence of Claude and Suzanne's artistry while also responding to it in a wholly original manner. The play's music and soundscape were composed and performed by Scottie Irving, who in the role of the Bandleader played the music live onstage with seven instruments and interacted with the other two performers. In production, instruments included piano, snare drum, harp, synthesizer, and accordion. I hope that future directors will use my stage directions as suggestions to create new surrealistic and imagistic playgrounds for the characters. Lastly, although the play is based on historical characters and historical events, *Heartlines* is a work of fiction, and any inaccuracies are either my intention or my fault.

PRODUCTION STILLS

Scottie Irving as the Bandleader and Margo MacDonald as Claude in *Heartlines*, 2022: set and props design by Andrea Steinwand, costume design by Vanessa Imeson, lighting design by Tristan-Olivier Breiding, video design by Kim Kölle Valentine, photo by Andrew Alexander

Margo MacDonald as Claude in *Heartlines*, 2022: set and props design by Andrea Steinwand, costume design by Vanessa Imeson, lighting design by Tristan-Olivier Breiding, video design by Kim Kölle Valentine, photo by Andrew Alexander

Maryse Fernandes as Suzanne and Margo MacDonald as Claude in *Heartlines*, 2022: set and props design by Andrea Steinwand, costume design by Vanessa Imeson, lighting design by Tristan-Olivier Breiding, video design by Kim Kölle Valentine, photo by Andrew Alexander

Maryse Fernandes as Suzanne in *Heartlines*, 2022: set and props design by Andrea Steinwand, costume design by Vanessa Imeson, lighting design by Tristan-Olivier Breiding, video design by Kim Kölle Valentine, photo by Andrew Alexander

ACT 1

PROLOGUE

In Suzanne's memory, CLAUDE is swimming in the sea. In the present, SUZANNE unpacks an old trunk and finds a notebook, which she opens to read.

SUZANNE
"Is there anything more powerful than first love? Anything so potent as that first kiss?" Remember? How all the blood from your body rushed into your mouth, your ears, your groin, your cheeks ... until then I had never felt that tingling in my fingers and the lightness in my head ... it's miserable but pleasurable and weird ... remember? The softness of your lips. The saltiness. And then your tongue – in my mouth – yes, stay there – don't stop doing that – keep doing that – what are you doing to me? That feels so ... that feels so ... that first kiss taunted me until, finally, I felt your whole body at once under my body, under my hands, under my mouth, under my tongue ... I never forgot that first kiss.

CLAUDE beckons to SUZANNE.

CLAUDE
The water's wonderful. Why don't you come in?

SUZANNE
You always say that. And it's always freezing!

CLAUDE
I'm going to drag you in if you don't come in yourself!

SUZANNE
Don't you dare!

CLAUDE emerges playfully from the water and strikes a pose reminiscent of one of the photos from the "I am in training don't kiss me!" series.

SCENE 1

A YOUTHFUL PASSION

SUZANNE

I was the older girl. But she seduced me. We were at the lycée together in Nantes. She was two years younger. I knew she was Jewish and that her family owned the local newspaper. She claimed she had been paying attention to me. Watching me. She always said she pursued me in such a way that I couldn't refuse. Typical Claude.

CLAUDE

I always knew. Most people know from a young age, not necessarily that they love women, or men if they're men, but they know they're different. For me it was like a thirst I couldn't quench. My earliest happy memory is of holding my cousin Marie's hand and walking with her in a field. I never forgot that warmth, that softness. When I met Suzanne, I already knew what I wanted from her because I had felt it with Marie when we held hands, and I had felt it again a few years later when Marie and I moved on to exploring each other's bodies. She wanted to practise making babies, and so we did the best we could with what we had ... so I knew what orgasm felt like even though my technique had been, up until then, largely accidental, and my liaisons had been limited to my cousin. Of course it was forbidden. It was a sin for the Catholics. But for the Jews? I always found their opinion about gay women much less clear. Not that I was religious. Unless it suited me. Which is, some would say, very Jewish.

SUZANNE

Suddenly, there she was one afternoon in the school's art studio: Mademoiselle Lucy Schwob. I asked her if she painted. She said no. "Why are you here, then?" I asked. "To meet you. Will you teach me to paint?" And so I taught her all I knew.

CLAUDE

I wanted her to know my name. And then I wanted to steal a kiss. A quick bisou. On the mouth.

SUZANNE

We quickly became inseparable. I was asked to tutor her in painting as well as in German because I was fluent – my family always spoke German at home – but Lucy was not all that interested in the finer points of technique in either art or grammar ... eventually, when my widowed mother announced she would marry her widowed father, we became stepsisters, and we laughed and laughed ...

SCENE 2
DRAWING LESSONS

CLAUDE and SUZANNE are adolescents. They both have sketching paper and pencils all around them. They are sketching the landscape before them; it is an outdoor drawing lesson.

SUZANNE
How is it going? Don't forget to use more contrast this time for the shadows.

CLAUDE
Shhh ... you're distracting me.

SUZANNE
Are you ready to show me what you have?

CLAUDE
Pas encore. Not yet.

CLAUDE is not sketching the landscape.

SUZANNE
Lucy, half the work of drawing is looking ... you need to look carefully at what you are drawing ...

CLAUDE looks at SUZANNE.

SUZANNE
What on earth are you up to?

SUZANNE snatches CLAUDE's notebook to look at it.

CLAUDE
Merde! It was going to be a surprise – this meadow is boring. I thought I would draw us instead.

SUZANNE

I don't see any figures in that sketch.

CLAUDE

Look closer, ma chère. We are both there. In the lips – I've written my name: Lucy Schwob. In the eye, your name: Suzanne Malherbe. And our initials spell out "elles s'aiment." Tu vois? El ... ess ... em ... Lucy Schwob Suzanne Malherbe. L.S.M. Elles – s'aiment –

SUZANNE

I see ... but why did you draw a hand? What does the shoe mean?

CLAUDE

You keep me grounded – or else I would fly away. And yet the hand is reaching high above.

SUZANNE

I like the detail in the hand. Hands are difficult to draw.

CLAUDE

I wanted to show how we're beshert. Fated. I feel like you're part of me, like the lines in my hand, like the lines of fate in my hand.

SUZANNE

Like lifelines.

CLAUDE

Like lifelines.

SUZANNE

L.S.M. Elles s'aiment ... (*confessing*) I love you, Lucy.

CLAUDE

I hope you do. Because I love you. L.S.M. Elles s'aiment. It's a code – our secret code. I'm going to write those letters all over town, and you'll know it's for you.

SUZANNE
Oh yeah? Where exactly?

CLAUDE
I was thinking I would start with the synagogue, then the school, then all the churches, then your mother's house, etc. This way you will be blushing terribly in public all the time, each time you see it, because it will remind you that I love you, and also that I want to kiss you, and fuck you ...

SUZANNE
You're terrible! People will talk!

CLAUDE
So what if they talk? I love you, and I want everyone to know.

SUZANNE
Lucy, you know that's not possible. But I love you too. Just ... more quietly ... in any case, draw me that meadow like you were supposed to!

SUZANNE returns the notebook, but CLAUDE drops it to the ground and approaches SUZANNE. They slowly move closer and closer together. This is SUZANNE's first kiss.

SCENE 3

OUTSIDER

In this scene, CLAUDE changes clothes from a girl's skirt to pants, shirt, men's shoes, and coat; these have been on a dressmaker's mannequin onstage since the top of the show.

CLAUDE

If you've always felt *normal*, then you can't begin to understand what it feels like to know you are Other. Different. Eventually in Paris I met other women and men who never felt like they belonged: they were Jews, Blacks, queers. Often they were artists. They kept travelling, kept running, kept performing, kept writing – always on the fringes no matter where they landed. But there will always be someone who refuses to hide, who refuses to wear a skirt or be married off. For me, it's like my body never matched me. As a girl I tried to match me to my body, but it felt like the inside of my head was on fire every time I acted like a good little girl. So to stop the feeling of the fire in my head, I stopped trying to match me to my body: I wore a girl's school uniform, but I wore tzitzit under my blouse, put a kippah on my head ... I wanted to be like the Jewish boys at religious school, learn what they were learning ... but it got me in trouble. First it was just teasing from those boys, and then one day some goyish kids tied me to a tree and pelted me with rocks. After that my father sent me to boarding school in England. But I got into a different kind of trouble there, and I was dragged home to go to the local lycée. That's when I met Suzanne.

The ultimate betrayal was my own body. How would I stop that bleeding every month? I couldn't believe how wasteful it was: all that blood and pain and I knew even then that I never wanted to be a mother, never wanted a man near me. But my breasts, my hips, my belly, my thighs ... so soft and rounded – as if to spite me. I wondered how thin I would have to get until my woman's body disappeared. I knew I could make my breasts disappear under tight bandages or cloth, but how could I get rid of them forever? Don't get me wrong: I didn't want to be a man. I just didn't want to be a woman. Could I be neither? I didn't want a prick, I just didn't want to live in this soft body – I never did. Was there another option? A third option? The space and possibility of a third sex excited me. An in-between space between man and woman. A third sex. Neuter. Not feminine or masculine. Not femme or homme but neutre. That's what I knew I was. And I was certain there were others like me. But in Nantes? I felt utterly alone. Even after I met Suzanne.

SUZANNE

The smell of the salt in the air. The cry of the seagulls. That was Brittany. But actually in Nantes we were inland, locked in the city, and I had to wait for holidays to go to the water. When I was young, I always dreamed of sailing into sunsets saturated with colour: orange, vivid purples, rose, reds that met the sea. I painted these sea sunsets in my mind and on paper before I ever saw them. I yearned for them, for that taste of salt. Later, I realized that it was those sea sunsets that made me yearn for God – but not the Catholic God I was raised to fear. It was Claude's God I wanted to know.

SCENE 4

A NEW BEGINNING

In this scene, props, clothing, art and writing supplies, and a camera emerge from the trunk to create the Parisian apartment of CLAUDE and SUZANNE.

SUZANNE
Inevitably, we left Nantes.

CLAUDE
It was only a matter of time.

SUZANNE
We moved to Paris. We lived there for seventeen years.

CLAUDE
I had to leave Nantes. I would have died otherwise.

SUZANNE
It was so we could study art properly.

CLAUDE
And be together properly.

SUZANNE
And study philosophy and literature. I threw myself into design and drawing, while you took up writing and theatre. And we both began to explore photography. I hoped Paris would be an ideal place for us to –

CLAUDE
– love each other properly.

SUZANNE
And grow into ourselves as artists and as intellectuals –

CLAUDE
– and as lovers.

SUZANNE
But also as artists. *Silly.* It was then that we decided to choose pen names.

CLAUDE
You picked Marcel Moore, and I chose Claude Cahun – androgynous names –

SUZANNE
– or else no one would have ever looked at our work: my drawings, your writing, our photographs. I picked Marcel for your uncle: everyone needs a Gay Jewish Uncle.

CLAUDE
Just so. And I picked Cahun for my more obscure Jewish relatives – all those rabbis. Cahun. Like Cohen.

SUZANNE
Cohen means your family were priests in ancient times. See: you *are* neglecting your responsibilities by choosing art.

CLAUDE
Making sacrifices and running the temple? Only if you were a man.

SUZANNE
Right. As usual.

CLAUDE
Is it time?

SUZANNE
It's time.

Introductory musical flourish.

CLAUDE
Welcome to our home!

SUZANNE
Bienvenue chez nous!

CLAUDE
Welcome to our bedroom carnival! We have a special presentation for you tonight, and then we promise there will be more dancing! And more drinking!

SUZANNE opens some champagne and pours glasses, perhaps even for the first row of the audience.

CLAUDE
We want to share a new piece of writing that we wrote together, and therefore it's a little different from my usual work, which you've been kind enough to suffer through before. This piece is a duet! A two-hander. It might be terrible, but we're going to try it out on you now, providing you've had enough champagne.

CLAUDE and SUZANNE toast.

CLAUDE
May we present:

CLAUDE and SUZANNE
An Ode to Paris.

SUZANNE
By Marcel and Claude.

CLAUDE
By Claude and Marcel.

CLAUDE
(*to the BANDLEADER*) Maestro? Some music if you please ...

Musical flourish.

CLAUDE

Our days in Paris were magnificent. Paris was impossible not to love in those days. Everyone was there.

"The Star-Spangled Banner" plays.

SUZANNE

American writers and American queers.

CLAUDE

Bonjour. Je suis an American in Paris. Je m'appelle Gertrude Stein. No, Stein, not *Shteen*, Stein. I am *very famous* in America! That's Alice.

"Rule, Britannia!" or "God Save the King" plays.

CLAUDE

British writers – mostly queers.

SUZANNE

Cheerio, Radclyffe Hall here, pleasure to meet you. John to my friends. But *we* aren't friends yet. Question: does everyone always greet each other so ... *intimately* here *all the time* ... No, no, no, I didn't order wine, I ordered tea. TEA! Harumph. France!

Tchaikovsky's "Swan Theme" plays.

SUZANNE

Russian princesses – often queers.

CLAUDE

Spaziba: your most expensive vodka and caviar, s'il vous plait, garçon. Now. Now. Here now. Now. Here now. Here. Now ... oh là là, you are cute. We fuck now, yes?

Lively "Hava Nagila" or other Jewish folk tune plays.

SUZANNE

Russian Jews – mostly penniless painters.

CLAUDE groans miserably, head in hands.

SUZANNE

Soutine! Are you ever going to pay your tab? You owe me two hundred francs! Who do you think you are, the next Chagall?!

CLAUDE

Would you take a painting of a rotting beef carcass? It's all I have ...

SUZANNE

Ah! Les artistes!

CLAUDE groans.

Concluding musical flourish.

CLAUDE

Paris – la ville lumière. Everybody wanted to be there. The foreigners came all at once, for the season, and acted as if the cafés belonged to *them*. They didn't notice that while, yes, this is where we drank and flirted with them and watched life go by, this was also where we planned and plotted against capitalism, slavery, the government increasingly turning fascist! Paris was our lover and our war room. The city vibrated with energy. It was ... sexy.

SUZANNE

Each morning felt like a new world. When I couldn't sleep, I got up early and went out into the city. Claude liked to sleep in and wake up only in time for lunch, but I loved the mornings. I knew the bakers and the whores and those who opened their bistros early ... I walked for hours. Sometimes I followed the Seine as far as I could – I knew it would eventually lead me to the sea, if only I could walk that far – I loved the stillness and the calm of Paris just waking up. I loved our nights too, but somehow the days were hard work.

CLAUDE
Nice to hear you say you loved our nights. Paris at night: nothing better –

SUZANNE
– but the mornings for stillness. If I could have had it my way, I would have skipped over the days entirely and moved from the half-light of dawn to the half-light of dusk, ignoring the rest.

SUZANNE
(*to CLAUDE, overlapping*) It was the mornings I loved.

CLAUDE
(*to SUZANNE, overlapping*) I loved Paris at night ...

CLAUDE
Maybe for you, Suzanne, but not for me. *Non*, it was the *night*! Paris was at her best at night! (*to the BANDLEADER*) You remember, mon ami! You were there too! The scandals, the champagne, the dancing –

The BANDLEADER and CLAUDE sing the (anachronistic) song "Sous le ciel de Paris" together.

CLAUDE
How many times did we fall asleep in each other's arms on a park bench or on the cobblestone streets? "America is my country and Paris is my hometown," said Gertrude, and on this point we agreed. We all loved Paris fiercely – and we would have killed to defend it, even as it drove us mad.

SUZANNE
People came from everywhere to live here. Remember Eli? He was a lover of Nadja's at first. He was here without any money, a Jew from Seville. He was the most beautiful man, and

Claude and I ... well, even we danced with him a few times, and somehow he managed to get Claude quite flustered –

CLAUDE
– a Spanish Adonis –

SUZANNE
– he lived at La Ruche with the other poor foreign artists. Then suddenly he was gone, and Nadja came crying to us and said he had left her for a German actor who had just played in the cabaret we had seen the week before. They went to Berlin. *I* wouldn't want to go there – this Hitler sounds like a real fanatic, wouldn't you agree?

Music stops abruptly.

And he certainly doesn't like queers. Or Jews. Or queer Jews!

Music only resumes when CLAUDE continues the narrative.

CLAUDE
Everyone wants to live in Montparnasse with its ateliers and cafés. If you are bored or frustrated with your own work, all you need to do is walk to Le Dôme and order a coffee or some wine, and next to you will be an actress you admire who you can fawn over until you forget your own troubles: Bonjour, Mademoiselle. I know you. You played last week at La Comédie. My name is Cahun. Claude. I'd like to photograph you. May I sit? ... Montparnasse! Forget Montmartre! Only Picasso is still there, and for how long? It is from here in Montparnasse that Paris will delight and shock the world, especially America. It is from here that true liberty will be fought for and come to be – Vive Contre-Attaque! Vive la liberté!

Musical flourish: CLAUDE starts to bow, but SUZANNE interrupts – she has perhaps had too much champagne ...

SUZANNE

But life in Paris can be hard. When the sky is as grey as the Seine, sometimes I think about throwing myself into the water, floating my way to the sea. And then the only question is from which bridge? There are so many to choose from.

Music fades out.

CLAUDE and SUZANNE recover and smile for the audience. They take their bows. SUZANNE returns to the bottle of champagne.

CLAUDE

(*aside*) I hate it when you talk like that. You can be so ... morbid.

SUZANNE

Give me a break ... It's just a play.

CLAUDE

I swear, Suzanne, this is the last time we perform together. You can't just go off book like that.

SUZANNE

This was supposed to be a collaboration, NOT one of your solos. I was collaborating.

CLAUDE

You were going rogue. If there is a next time, we will do one of my scripts. No more co-writing.

SUZANNE

You need to be in control all the time, don't you? *You're* not famous yet, for all your ego. You haven't exhibited or published a thing!

CLAUDE

But I will. And when I do, it will be a sensation.

SUZANNE

Well, when you do, I demand co-credit.

CLAUDE

You know the portraits are more impressive if it seems like I did them alone.

SUZANNE

They are already impressive!

CLAUDE

Yes, but as autoportraiture ... as the work of a single auteur ...

SUZANNE

If the design is mine, or the shot or the composition is mine, then it's not an autoportrait, it's a collaboration, and you know it.

CLAUDE

I thought you didn't want to be in the spotlight! Come on, Suzanne! Think about it – think about how astounding the portraits are as the work of a *solo* artist – you can still help me to make them – but if they are exhibited, it will be as by Cahun ... as done by Claude Cahun, *alone* ...

SUZANNE

You're impossible. Do what you want. But don't come crying to me if someone accuses you of being a fraud.

SCENE 5
AUTOPORTRAITURE

CLAUDE

(*setting up the camera*) Autoportraiture is not a selfish, egotistical whimsy. It is practical. It is simpler to use myself rather than someone else, c'est tout. I think Suzanne is jealous that she is not my muse. But she is my everything else. Isn't that enough? I do not have a muse, because I do not need one. Why is she jealous of that?

Autoportraiture is very technical. I said it was simpler and it is, emotionally, because you don't have to consider the needs of the model, but it does require the precision of the instruments, the lighting, and above all the timing. So in those respects, it can be difficult to do well. But the liberty is unparalleled.

There is no one to get in the way of the shot I want to get.

I had a muse once. Vanessa. Her given name was Esther, but she took on Vanessa to make herself sound *exotic.* I thought she was gorgeous, ravissante. Such long limbs – always entwined around some piece of furniture or around themselves. You couldn't help but imagine her legs wrapped around your own body. And when we made love, it was like that: all legs, all arms, all writhing and tangled limbs, sweaty, musky, athletic sex. Nothing tender about us. Vanessa was as strong as she was long, and she liked to compete with me for power. We fought it out in her bed, in stairwells, in a park once in the dead of night.

Vanessa. I painted her. I painted her skin too, once, and arranged her body against a blank canvas. Then I told her to move as if she were making love to me. I stayed back and watched her move alone on the virgin canvas until it was covered in paint and sweat, and we were both spent. Just watching her brought me to orgasm. I had never felt so done in before, so undone.

SUZANNE

(*absorbed in her work on the easel*) It was fine with me when Claude went out. I liked having quiet to draw and to think, to be alone in our tiny apartment with my thoughts and my pencils. I liked to host, but I preferred when others did, like the rich American Natalie Barney with her Friday salons on rue Jacob, near our flat. Natalie was known as L'Amazone but I used to call her La Lesbienne, because she was *Not Interested in Hiding It*, and she made it clear that Claude and I had an open invitation to her salon. Sometimes I sent Claude to Natalie's for a few days so I could work in peace and quiet. This was my ideal version of a ménage à trois: everyone was satisfied.

SCENE 6

INACCROCHABLE ("IT WILL NEVER SELL")

SUZANNE is cutting out images and moving them around on her easel. CLAUDE storms into the apartment.

CLAUDE
Suzanne! Suzanne! Adrienne Monnier doesn't want it. She said it would never sell. "Inaccrochable," she said, quoting Gertrude! Can you believe it? And they say they can't stand each other! La vache!

SUZANNE
Slow down, please.

CLAUDE
I showed Adrienne the manuscript like we talked about, and she doesn't want to publish it. She doesn't want to publish *Disavowals.*

SUZANNE
I'm so sorry, sweetheart. I thought for sure she would want it. Maybe it needs a little more work?

CLAUDE
I thought it was ready. I feel so stupid. Adrienne said the writing was strong but that it was too "opaque" and "confusing," that the reader would have to work too hard. But that's the whole point! I *want* them to work! I want the reader to be challenged by the structure, by the ambiguity – otherwise it's just a novel! I argued with Adrienne about that, saying I wasn't interested in tradition, in being the next Balzac, and *then* she suggested I try my hand at a journal intime! A tell-all memoir?! I couldn't believe it! Shiksa cow. She didn't even catch the Yom Kippur reference in the title. She's a philistine.

Journal intime?! That's fake writing for and by little old ladies ... I'm done with her, with Sylvia Beach, with their conjoined-twin bookstores, with everything ... For my revenge I'm going to seduce Gertrude and Alice both and be a social pariah and write opaque novels in invisible ink, since my writing is so unsellable.

SUZANNE
Makes sense.

CLAUDE
Do you think my book is too weird? ... I'm going to make the book even weirder, then. So weird no one will want to read it, let alone buy it.

SUZANNE
Mmmhhmm. You do that, sweetheart.

CLAUDE
You're not even listening to me! What are you working on that is so important?

SUZANNE
(*SUZANNE finally looks up to CLAUDE and softens)* I'm sorry. I'm just playing with that technique of Picasso and Braque's – collage – with some cuttings of our photographs – and seeing what happens if the pieces are assembled randomly, like the images in a kaleidoscope when you turn the barrel. Remember those toys? The shapes in the toy are geometric, but what if they weren't? What if they were motifs from our photographs? How can they keep changing and transforming on the page?

CLAUDE
You are brilliant, my love. Collage. I love this! The images don't make sense together – but in a way they do? Wait – does each collage have a central theme, or is it entirely random? How did you choose what goes together? Tell me everything! Wait! I hereby commission you to illustrate my unpublishable, unsellable, inaccrochable book. I want you to make me the most confusing, unique, mutant illustrations possible. We'll never sell

any books, but to hell with it. And then we'll bestow a signed copy to Adrienne with thanks for the inspiration. She can share it with Sylvia. That cow.

CLAUDE sweeps SUZANNE off her feet, and they dance around the apartment, laughing, mooing, and scattering all the collage material.

SCENE 7

WORKING WITH MODELS

Towards the end of a long photography session. CLAUDE is wearing a sleeveless shirt and jacket. SUZANNE is in regular house clothes, including a skirt or a kimono. SUZANNE is posing for CLAUDE, who is behind the camera. Her pose echoes Autoportrait, *ca. 1928 (Claude with shaved head and sleeveless shirt).*

CLAUDE
Why won't you keep still?

SUZANNE
I have been sitting here for a long time, Monsieur le photographe, and I have a cramp.

CLAUDE
Well, stretch a bit and then be still, for God's sake, or we'll miss the shot.

SUZANNE
I've been holding this pose for hours while you find the perfect light. Can I ever be more than simply your object, Monsieur?

CLAUDE
Shut up, Suzanne. You are Marcel Moore, my esteemed collaborator. But for this session, you are merely my placeholder, not my model. Now be still, for God's sake.

SUZANNE
Or else what?

CLAUDE
You are really trying my patience today – why is that? Just one minute and I'll almost have it. Don't move!

They are both still for thirty seconds while CLAUDE finds the light.

CLAUDE
Okay! Good. Now let me in there.

They switch places. CLAUDE takes on the pose SUZANNE has just held. There is something luminescent when CLAUDE models.

CLAUDE
Now! Take the photo!

Silence as CLAUDE freezes and SUZANNE expertly takes the photo.

CLAUDE
Good. Now come here. Please.

Pause.

What's the problem? You've had nothing but attitude all afternoon. What's wrong?

SUZANNE
I don't like your ... look.

CLAUDE
You don't like my "look"?

SUZANNE
Non.

CLAUDE
(*laughing*) It's just a shirt, Suzanne, which *you* made for me. This "look" is *your* design which you dreamed up in one of your nightmare *visions*.

SUZANNE
Yes, but you look ... more ... frightening ... than I expected. You look like a prisoner. I don't like it. Why did you have to cut your hair so short?

CLAUDE
I thought you liked my hair short.

SUZANNE
Not that short.

CLAUDE
Is that really what's bothering you? What exactly is your problem today? (*mockingly, tongue in cheek*) Oh, I know what's going on. You think I get to have all the fun while you toil away in obscurity with your drawing. But it's not all fun and games, ma chérie. I am Claude Cahun. I am a visionary. But fine, if you think you want to pose for me, really pose for me, you'll have to wear a costume too.

CLAUDE takes off SUZANNE's skirt or kimono and gives her a soldier's coat.

SUZANNE
Fine.

Pause.

(*giving CLAUDE a skirt*) Now you put this on.

CLAUDE
Non.

SUZANNE
Do it.

CLAUDE puts on the skirt and curtsies.

SUZANNE
Now you photograph me.

SUZANNE mockingly takes up a pose from the "I am in training don't kiss me!" series.

CLAUDE
I would rather fuck you.

SUZANNE
Too bad. Take my photo.

CLAUDE takes a photo. SUZANNE strikes another pose, playing as CLAUDE in I am in training don't kiss me. *CLAUDE approaches SUZANNE.*

SUZANNE
Arrête! ... don't come any closer ... I said: Take my photo!

CLAUDE returns to the camera and looks through it as SUZANNE takes a pose she knows will arouse CLAUDE. CLAUDE takes another picture but then ... they can't keep away from each other.

SCENE 8

VIVE LA FRANCE

SUZANNE and CLAUDE are listening to the radio, which plays a live broadcast. The voice on the radio builds in intensity from urgent to bellicose.

RADIO
(*voiceover*) This is the BBC for August 5, 1929. Herr Hitler and his Nationalist Socialist "nazi" Party held their fourth party congress in Nuremberg, Germany, from August first to fourth –

SUZANNE
Fucking nazis.

CLAUDE
A *fourth* congress?

RADIO
(*voiceover*) This fourth rally was given the name "The Day of Composure" –

SUZANNE
How poetic.

RADIO
(*voiceover*) – a fireworks show enthralled the crowd of attendees, including Great War hero General Van Epp –

CLAUDE
Whoever that is.

SUZANNE
Are you sure we shouldn't leave? We could go to America.

CLAUDE
We don't know anyone there. Besides, they hate queers and Jews and Blacks in America, just like in Germany.

SUZANNE

Antarctica then. Canada. Palestine. This is ridiculous! He's a madman.

CLAUDE

The Germans elected him.

SUZANNE

Then they're all equally mad.

RADIO

(*voiceover*) – French Jewish communities as well as scholars and intellectuals are pressuring the government to intervene, but sources say l'Élysée would rather not repeat the Dreyfus affair ...

CLAUDE

Next he will go after the queers and the Blacks and the communists. Like always. Hitler hates all of us – and he's not even hiding it anymore!

SUZANNE

(*spitting*) Don't say his name in this house.

CLAUDE

Someone should shoot him. Before he does any more damage.

SUZANNE

What if they have someone worse than Hitler waiting in the wings?

CLAUDE

(*spitting*) God forbid.

SUZANNE

Fuck you, Hitler!

CLAUDE

(*making a Hitler moustache with a finger between nose and lip*) You didn't salute, soldier.

SUZANNE

(*also making a Hitler moustache*) Verzeihung, mein Kapitän. I beg your pardon, mein Herr.

CLAUDE

(*clicking heels, giving a mockery of the nazi salute*) Heil Hitler! Long live das Vaterland!

SUZANNE

Nein! Long live die Mutterland: Vive la France!

CLAUDE

Heil la France! Heil l'Alsace et la Lorraine!

SUZANNE

Heil Paris! Heil Montparnasse! Heil les gaies Parisiennes!

CLAUDE

Heil Claude Cahun! Heil Marcel Moore!

CLAUDE and SUZANNE mock goose-step around the apartment. Each has a hand raised as a moustache, the other arm raised in salute. The radio broadcast gets louder and merges with their salutes.

CLAUDE

Heil les Deux Magots!

SUZANNE

Heil Café de Flore!

CLAUDE

Heil James Joyce!

SUZANNE

Heil Sylvia Beach!

CLAUDE

Heil André Breton!

SUZANNE
Heil Picasso!

CLAUDE
Heil les Folies Bergère!

SUZANNE
Heil Josephine Baker!

CLAUDE
Heil Gertrude Stein!

SUZANNE
Heil la Ville Lumière!

The sound of metal-tipped boots increases in intensity as the radio volume increases.

Transition to interlude. CLAUDE and SUZANNE listen to the next broadcast.

RADIO
(*voiceover*) This is the BBC World Service on the 3rd of September 1939. This is London. You will now hear a message from the Prime Minister of Great Britain: "This morning the British Ambassador in Berlin handed the German government a final note stating that unless we heard from them by eleven o'clock that they were prepared at once to withdraw their troops from Poland, a state of war would be declared by us ... consequently this country is at war with Germany. I repeat: this country is at war with Germany."

CLAUDE and SUZANNE kiss each other in deliberate defiance to the rising nazi tide.

Lights go out suddenly. End of Act 1.

ACT 2

PROLOGUE

RADIO

(*voiceover*) This is the BBC World Service. In April 1940 Germany invades Denmark and Norway. On the 10th of May 1940, Winston Churchill is appointed Prime Minister of Great Britain. On the same day, as a token of their congratulations, Germany invades northeastern France, sweeping past the Maginot Line and through the Ardennes Forest to also take Belgium, the Netherlands, and Luxembourg. On the 14th of June 1940, our beautiful Paris falls to the nazis. Collaboration becomes a dirty word. France is now under occupation by Germany and its ally Italy. On the 28th of June 1940, German squadrons bomb the harbours of the tiny islands of Guernsey and Jersey in the English Channel. Forty-three islanders are killed. On the 30th of June 1940, Guernsey and Jersey surrender to the German army. Occupation is declared. In September 1940, relentless bombing begins on London and other cities in Britain in what will become known as the Blitz. In Jersey today it is below seasonal but sunny. Ten years have passed since we last saw our protagonists. They are no longer quite so young but just as, ahem, queer as ever ...

SCENE 1
AWAY TO JERSEY

SUZANNE and CLAUDE have left the freedom of Paris behind, and they are now both dressed in 1940s skirts, sweaters, and headscarves.

CLAUDE
It was Suzanne's idea to go to Jersey. I didn't want to leave Paris. But in 1937, we did.

SUZANNE
That's a lie. It was *your* idea to go to Jersey. Everyone we knew was trying to leave Paris. We could have gone to Italy with Natalie or gone to America with her sister – but you wanted to not be too far from Paris – and Jersey seemed far enough away from Berlin and that madman.

CLAUDE
I thought we would be safe here. No one knew us on Jersey as Jews or as lovers – we were just eccentric, middle-aged artists.

SUZANNE
And it was fine at first for Claude to wear trousers. Before the war our friends visited us regularly – just a train ride and ferry from Paris ... and we got a cat!

CLAUDE
That's true. We got the first of our several cats. Each of them was called Kid. And each of them learned to walk on a leash.

SUZANNE
And Jersey was beautiful. You loved our house. We named it La ferme inconnue. It had a terrace, and a garden, and we could walk to the sea. Remember? We would take the cat with us and go to the beach every day to see the sunset. The water and the sky were all around us.

CLAUDE

We took marvellous photographs on Jersey. Suzanne had to make weekly visits to the druggist to develop the negatives. He blushed every time she came to pick them up!

SUZANNE

I went to sleep each night and woke up each morning with the sound of the crashing waves, with the smell of salt, with the wide-open sky above us, with Claude next to me in bed. We were safe.

CLAUDE

We were safe. For three years. And then nazi Germany came to us.

SUZANNE

I wanted to keep you safe.

CLAUDE

And I you.

SUZANNE

How could we know that les Boches would take Paris, make it all the way across France to Normandy and then across the Channel to Jersey, to this tiny speck of grass?

SCENE 2

AN ODE TO THE OCCUPATION

SUZANNE

May we present ...

SUZANNE and CLAUDE

An Ode to the Occupation!

Pause. SUZANNE and CLAUDE look at each other.

CLAUDE

(*making the moustache gesture*) By Adolf Hitler.

SUZANNE

(*to the BANDLEADER*) Maestro? Some music if you please?

Musical flourish.

SUZANNE

On patrol:

CLAUDE takes up the ridiculous goose-stepping from the end of Act 1 again, and SUZANNE clomps boots or a prop to make the sound of boots on the cobblestone street. They pretend to be German soldiers in the following clown scene.

SUZANNE

Guten Tag, Hans. Heil Hitler!

CLAUDE

Guten Tag, Franz. Heil Hitler!

SUZANNE

What shall we do today, Hans?

CLAUDE

I don't know, Franz. So many choices. Well, first we could arrest some people for no reason, then we could march around the village with our chests out really big and our legs very stiff – like so – and look very constipated.

SUZANNE

Ja, Hans, that is an idea most wunderbar.

CLAUDE

Prima! And then what shall we do after that, Franz?

SUZANNE

Then it will be time for a big sausage!

Musical flourish.

CLAUDE

Two villagers from Jersey meet on the road:

SUZANNE

Bonjour, Pierre.

CLAUDE

Bonjour, Jean.

SUZANNE

(*whispering*) Did you hear what happened to M. Le Claire? He tried to hide his pig Jojo so the officers wouldn't confiscate him, but then his neighbour – that busybody anglaise Mrs. Ross – denounced him! He hasn't been seen since!

CLAUDE

Jojo?

SUZANNE

No, imbecile, M. Le Claire! Jojo has been promoted to Kommandant.

SUZANNE snorts.

Musical flourish.

SUZANNE
A German soldier visits a villager's house:

CLAUDE
(*playing a soldier*) Knock knock. Heil Hitler! On orders from Berlin, from the Führer himself, Heil Hitler, you must turn in your radio, Heil Hitler, Heil Hitler!

SUZANNE
(*playing a middle-aged English woman*) Yes, yes, what you said. Here is my only radio, soldier.

CLAUDE
Gut. (*taking the radio brusquely*) Heil Hitler!

SUZANNE
Auf Wiedersehen!

As CLAUDE marches away, SUZANNE gives the soldier the finger. Then she pulls out a second radio, along with both a French flag and a Union Jack.

Musical flourish. CLAUDE and SUZANNE bow.

SCENE 3

AWAY TO JERSEY, BIS

SUZANNE

Some of the officers are charming to us, even friendly. It makes me nervous. I keep thinking it's a trick to pull information out of us, like about who is secretly a Jew. (*camping/mocking*) "My Catholic stepsister and I are being good little old ladies." I have no idea how long we can keep this up.

CLAUDE

So far, here on Jersey, "Occupation" means rigid politeness, a few shows of might, constantly changing curfews, the threat of random arrest, starvation, and illness, repossession and seizure of goods, no big deal.

SUZANNE

There are terrible rumours. People are disappearing in France now too.

CLAUDE

Nobody can tell me where Gertrude and Alice are, and I haven't heard from Vanessa since ... I don't know what's happened to Vanessa. Or to Eli and his boyfriend in Berlin.

SUZANNE

Resistance groups are forming. People are rising up, taking action.

CLAUDE

Not Jews. I'm sure it's not other Jews. Everyone's in hiding.

SUZANNE

We have to do something.

CLAUDE
We are artists. Our job is to make art.

SUZANNE
(*aside*) When the soldiers landed, I lost all my colours, all my senses. Just like that: I couldn't even smell the salt of the sea.

SCENE 4

ONEG SHABBAT / WHO'S AFRAID OF VIRGINIA WOOLF?

CLAUDE is fussing with some writing. SUZANNE is doing some mending. The lights flicker, then go out.

CLAUDE
Merde. Merde ...

SUZANNE strikes a match, which illuminates her lighting first one candle, then another in a second candlestick. It is very quiet.

SUZANNE
It's Friday.

CLAUDE
Hmm?

SUZANNE
It's Friday night.

SUZANNE extinguishes the match and sets it down. SUZANNE brings her hands together three times, then covers her eyes and sings the blessing quietly, quietly.

SUZANNE
Baruh atah adonay, eloheynu meleh ha'olam, asher kideshanu bemitzvotav vetzivanu lehadlik ner shel shabbat.

CLAUDE
Amen.

SUZANNE
Shabbat shalom.

CLAUDE

Shabbat shalom.

CLAUDE and SUZANNE bless each other. Then SUZANNE separates the candlesticks so it's less obvious what they are.

CLAUDE

(*stalling*) Suzanne, sweetie, I have some terrible news. I didn't know how to tell you earlier ...

SUZANNE

What happened?

CLAUDE

Virginia Woolf died. She took her own life. They say she didn't want to live through another bombing of London. She was afraid of going mad. It was on the news. Michelle told me when I was in the village. She heard it from Pierre, who heard it himself on Jean's hidden radio. We can listen for it later tonight ... I can't believe it. She just gave up.

Pause.

She was a coward. That was a cowardly thing to do.

SUZANNE

No. I don't believe that.

CLAUDE

She's just like us, Suzoleh – none of us can stand this war. What about Vita? And Leonard? He's *Jewish*! What will happen to him? And what about her writing? This means there won't be any more books – my God –

SUZANNE

But she was able to choose how and when to die. I envy her.

CLAUDE

Don't you dare talk like that. I won't have it. Our job is to live. Hitler wants us dead. Each day that we live is a wound to him.

SUZANNE
I couldn't live without you.

CLAUDE
I'm not going anywhere!

SUZANNE
Claude. Claude. Look me in the eyes. I couldn't live without you.

CLAUDE
Of course you could, chérie.

SUZANNE
Never. It will only ever be you. If you were to die tomorrow, I couldn't manage. I would take my life like Virginia did.

CLAUDE
You're talking nonsense. I'm going to live until a hundred and twenty. However, if *you* died before me, I would –

The lights flicker back on.

– take it as a great opportunity to get rid of all your excessive sewing supplies and ridiculous bags of useless cloth, and then I would find a beautiful, fresh young lover to cook and clean for me – it would be just fine.

SUZANNE
You're impossible! Anyway, you know very well those bags of cloth have been pillaged by everyone up and down the street already. And a lover! Ha. Your fantasy assumes the end of the Occupation ... Virginia Woolf – how did she die?

CLAUDE
(*beat*) She put rocks in her pockets and jumped down into the river. It's terrible. She must have been very afraid. I'm so sorry she's dead.

SCENE 5

TWO HARD LINES

A lonely moment in the middle of the night.

CLAUDE

We don't make love anymore. Not since the Occupation began. I think I want to, as a distraction or a lark, but I can't summon the energy, and neither can she. In bed our bodies are two cold hard lines. If we hold each other, it's for warmth and because we are frightened. She's too skinny, and she tells me I am too. But actually I like how it's taking away my breasts and belly, little by little, this hunger. I will look more and more manly, less and less like a woman, if this keeps up. Hitler is starving the feminine out of me, it turns out. It makes me laugh to think he is getting the opposite of what he wants. But Suzanne is too thin and too cold. Her body reminds me of her body when we first met, but instead of desire, now it just fills me with loss. Maybe this is why we don't make love anymore. Her body looks like the body of a child, barely a teenager. I'm not sure she realizes how much this war has changed her. Now in bed I feel I am protecting a little girl. As if I can save either of us from anything.

SCENE 6

IT'S JUST A DRAWING

The sound of drips or leaking. The electric lights are working again. CLAUDE is writing in a notebook; SUZANNE is drawing. The following three scenes echo each other; the house should feel increasingly claustrophobic.

SUZANNE
What are you writing?

CLAUDE
Nothing.

SUZANNE
Well, don't waste paper on nothing. It's unseemly.

CLAUDE
What are *you* working on?

SUZANNE
Nothing. (*beat*) Just a silly drawing.

CLAUDE
You haven't drawn in ages. What is it? Show me.

SUZANNE
I'm not sure – Attends! –

CLAUDE takes hold of the paper.

CLAUDE
What exactly is this?

SUZANNE
It's just a brouillon. Give it back.

CLAUDE

No, not yet. Let me look … what does this German phrase mean? Does that say "pigs"?

SUZANNE

Translated it means "Go home to your squealing mommies, little pigs …"

CLAUDE

(*laughing*) I hope you plan to destroy that.

SUZANNE

I will. Only I had another of those dreams last night. This time I dreamed that the officers tried to raise up their hideous swastika flag at their HQ, and instead what came up was our Tricolore. The one we hid in the latrine. In my dream I was the one who had switched the flags.

CLAUDE

You wouldn't.

SUZANNE

I won't actually do that, Claude. But can't we do *something*?

CLAUDE

We *are* doing something. Our job is to *not* get arrested.

SUZANNE

That's not enough. I'm sick of doing nothing. I don't want to ration paper anymore. I don't want to eat soup made from vegetable skins or worry that another of our friends has disappeared. People are being rounded up! Where the fuck are they being taken to?

CLAUDE

You need to keep your voice down. Do you think I don't know all that? But someone might hear you. We can't trust anyone anymore.

SUZANNE

What happened to all your bravado? You're telling me to keep my voice down? You? The one who used to dance all night on the street, drunk, singing with the musicians until you lost your voice? You, who dragged *me* into Contre-Attaque with all those arrogant men like Breton so you could wage surrealist battle on fascism – you want *me* to be quiet?

CLAUDE

You're not the one they're after. You're not the Jew.

SUZANNE is stung by this.

SUZANNE

I am a Jew too, inside, where it counts. And we're *both* disgusting homosexuals to them.

Pause.

CLAUDE

I know.

SUZANNE

I'm sick of doing nothing, Claude. If I were a man, I would sail to London right now and enlist with the Allies.

CLAUDE

Or join a band of resisters and blow up some train tracks.

SUZANNE

Or steal some guns.

CLAUDE

Or kill a German. Slit his throat.

SUZANNE

No.

CLAUDE

Just how far would you go, chérie?

SCENE 7

REPRISE

The sound of drips or leaking or ticking.

SUZANNE
What are you writing?

CLAUDE
Nothing.

SUZANNE
Well, don't waste paper on nothing. It's unseemly.

Pause. Sound of a drip.

SUZANNE
I had that dream again last night.

CLAUDE
The flag?

SUZANNE
Yeah.

Pause. Sound of a drip.

SUZANNE
I passed a soldier today on the high street. He looked so young, still a kid. And was he ever cute, with a little smile as he wished me bonjour ... why is he here? Why did he join the army? He seemed so sweet.

CLAUDE
Maybe so, but I wouldn't trust him.

SUZANNE

Oh, I don't trust him either. But it made me think – maybe a few of them just got swept up in the frenzy. Maybe they were poor and had no future. Maybe they love their country and got confused about how to show that love.

CLAUDE

But they're here. An occupying force. Looking to arrest or deport us.

SUZANNE

Could we convince them not to? Could we convince them to quit, leave, even stand up to Hitler?

CLAUDE

Impossible.

SUZANNE

Remember when we were in Contre-Attaque? The pamphlets, the leaflets – we passed those around Paris to convince people to join us. And some of them were funny!

CLAUDE

Like that cartoon you showed me with the pigs ... you think pamphlets could convince them to leave Jersey?

SUZANNE

Maybe. I bet they only hear Berlin-approved news. I bet they don't even know the truth.

CLAUDE

We could distribute bulletins telling them what's really happening: show them the truth.

SUZANNE

I could translate the news from the BBC into der Muttersprache. Type it all in German. Remind them that the Allies haven't given up, that Germany isn't invincible.

CLAUDE

Convince them to defect before it's too late ... it doesn't make sense that they all could be so ...

SUZANNE

But it would have to be just the two of us. We can't trust anyone. You said so yourself. It's not safe.

CLAUDE

I know. I know.

SCENE 8
RESISTANCE HQ

The sound grows.

SUZANNE
What are you writing?

CLAUDE
Nothing.

SUZANNE
Well, don't waste paper on nothing. It's unseemly.

CLAUDE
Okay then, what have you got?

SUZANNE
I think our best strategy is the angle of dissuasion – instead of persuasion. Not so much *propaganda* as ... I don't know what to call it. And you'll have to trust me on the German.

CLAUDE
Fine. Let's hear it.

SUZANNE
Okay, three options. First: "The Fatherland is bereft without us! Defect! Defect! Defect!"

CLAUDE
Too long.

SUZANNE
Okay ... second option: "Get the fuck off our island."

CLAUDE
Seriously?

SUZANNE

Of course not! (*beat*) But I keep having that dream –

CLAUDE

What about: "We're going down! Abandon ship!" and we sign it: "Le soldat inconnu" ... I like it. It has a certain ... flair.

SUZANNE

Le Soldat inconnu. Der Soldat ohne Namen. The Soldier with No Name.

CLAUDE

Admittedly, I do like your suggestion of "Get the fuck off our island."

SUZANNE

And then tomorrow we'll follow the serving staff into the mess hall and put these tracts under the plates. "What's for lunch today, Hans? Oh, a note!"

CLAUDE

You know how they keep having their funerals in *our* churchyard? I bet when they're not paying attention, we could put these on the windshields of their waiting cars.

SUZANNE

I like it.

CLAUDE

Let's do it.

SCENE 9
PAPER ROUTE

This is a silent clown ode or interlude or vaudeville bit. SUZANNE and CLAUDE, costumed as elderly women, deliver leaflets around the theatre as if doing so secretly in the village: carefully in the mess hall, under windshield wipers, slipping them into cigarette packages, etc., encouraging people to pass them along through the audience; the lazzis build in intensity and elaborateness. In the premiere production, the dressmaker's mannequin played a starring role in this scene (dressed in a German officer's uniform) and a paper drop was done from the ceiling, so propaganda leaflets rained down on the audience at the scene's climax.

SCENE 10
THE ATTACK

SUZANNE is waiting up for Claude. The house looks even more shabby than it did before. Electricity is off again; just two or three candles light the space. SUZANNE lights a candle. It is dark – past curfew, night – and Claude should be home by now. With each sound SUZANNE hears, she startles. CLAUDE enters.

SUZANNE
Mon amour! What happened? Oh my God.

CLAUDE
I'm fine, help me to sit down.

SUZANNE
You're not fine. Are you hurt? You're hurt.

CLAUDE
Don't shout. Please. I'm fine.

CLAUDE sits carefully on a chair. SUZANNE begins to undress CLAUDE, who is covered in bruises and blood. The undressing happens very slowly, by candlelight.

CLAUDE
Suzanne. Suzoleh ...

SUZANNE
Shh, sweetie. Please don't say anything. I'm going to bring some hot water and soap to wash you, okay?

CLAUDE
I don't want you to see.

SUZANNE
Let me.

SUZANNE returns with water and begins to bathe a now shivering CLAUDE, who can't speak.

SUZANNE
Shhh, shhh, shhh.

SUZANNE hums "À la claire fontaine" to stay calm.

CLAUDE
There were six of them, on patrol. They stopped me – they said it was past curfew, but it wasn't, it was still light out. They pushed me around and called me names. Bitch. Cunt. Dyke. Not Jew – they didn't guess that. Thank God. Then they forced themselves on me. They took turns. And then one beat me up because finally it was dark and it was past curfew then, and the others watched and laughed. Then they left me on the road.

SUZANNE
Shhh, shhh, sweetie ... mon amour, I've got you. Shh, shh, baby, I've got you.

CLAUDE begins to cry but can't; their silent cry becomes a wail in the music. The sound of boots on cobblestone streets mixes with the lullaby and the wail.

SCENE 11

LE SOLDAT INCONNU – DER SOLDAT OHNE NAMEN – THE SOLDIER WITH NO NAME

Six weeks later. The house is more claustrophobic. CLAUDE is sitting still in a chair, thinking. SUZANNE comes in from outside. Long, uncomfortable pause before SUZANNE speaks.

SUZANNE

You won't believe what I heard on the road. Apparently, even though I can barely believe it, the soldiers think there is a *gang* of resisters at work here on Jersey. Here!

CLAUDE

Why? Because of our shitty leaflets?

SUZANNE

Because of our *relentless* shitty leaflets! Because there has been so much propaganda and so many small acts of insurrection. They are going to search the woods to find the gang of resisters who they think must be hiding there. I was so shocked. It was hard not to react. But then they would have seen I understood their German.

CLAUDE

What did they say, exactly?

SUZANNE

They think we're an army. Well, not quite that. But more numerous than two little old ladies.

CLAUDE

Speak for yourself, ma chère.

SUZANNE
Well in any case, it's working. They're getting nervous.

CLAUDE
They'll be so pissed when they spend hours in the rain looking for us.

SUZANNE
I hope they don't actually come across any resisters and hurt them. While looking for us.

CLAUDE
They might. It's possible.

SUZANNE
But wouldn't we know of them?

CLAUDE
I don't know. Would they know of us? Did anyone see you when you overheard that conversation with the Germans? Did anyone see that you *understood*?

SUZANNE
I don't think so.

CLAUDE
Okay. Good. If they're beginning to get worried –

SUZANNE
It means it's working ...

CLAUDE
If only they would just fuck off.

SUZANNE
(*beat*) This is an opportunity to do something really big.

CLAUDE
There are two of us and a whole barracks full of them!

SUZANNE
And yet we've managed to get under their skin. They're nervous. And they think we're a whole gang. I bet they also think we're men.

CLAUDE
Probably.

SUZANNE
What if ... I disguise myself as a soldier and go listen to what they're planning ... infiltrate their HQ!

CLAUDE
Now you're going to become a spy?

SUZANNE
Observer, Claude. I want to *do* something. Make them pay for what they did to you ... you used to disguise yourself for years. It can't be that hard.

CLAUDE
You know that wasn't a disguise. *THIS* is a disguise!

SUZANNE
That's not what I mean! I mean you were convincing as a soldier. In your photographs and onstage you played any character – soldier, sailor – I watched you that whole time ... I could do it too.

CLAUDE is gutted by this betrayal.

CLAUDE
Suzanne, that wasn't just theatre for me. That wasn't just pretend. That was – is who I am – this is not.

SUZANNE
I didn't mean to ... suggest it wasn't important for you to wear men's clothes. But couldn't I do that, Claude? Disguise myself

as a German soldier and break in and listen to them? Couldn't I pretend to be one of them?

CLAUDE
Stop. Just stop ... disguise yourself? Five years of me being forced to wear this – this fucking skirt – being trapped like – an animal – have you forgotten who I am? Have you forgotten, Suzanne? Do you even know me? This has never been me.

SUZANNE
I didn't mean to – it wasn't about you –

CLAUDE
It's different for you. You are yourself either way, in pants or in a skirt. But I need to choose. I need to decide – for me – how I'm seen. Who I am in the world.

SUZANNE
None of us has that luxury anymore.

CLAUDE
You do! I'm the one who has a target on my back. I'm the Jew! And I'm the one who looks like – an *invert.* They attacked me! You could just – leave – fade into the countryside.

SUZANNE
Leave? Is that what you really want? You don't mean that. I have never left you, and I never will.

CLAUDE
Listen to me, Suzanne. You need to leave. I need you to go someplace safe – and forget your bullshit plan –

SUZANNE
You haven't even heard my plan.

CLAUDE
You have no plan! You would be discovered in a second! Suzanne. Look at yourself. The leaflets are one thing. It's been

dangerous doing just that. But breaking into the HQ? That's just madness. No one would ever believe you were a German soldier. You'd never pass. I forbid it.

SUZANNE
Claude – Claude ...

Pause.

CLAUDE
I'm the one who's going to do it.

SUZANNE
Do what? Be a German soldier?

CLAUDE
I'm going to switch the flag.

SUZANNE
What?

CLAUDE
Like in your dream. Don't you still dream of switching the flag, of getting rid of their swastika? I could change it to the Union Jack or the Tricolore –

SUZANNE
That is never going to work. Your German isn't good enough! The minute you spoke, you would be found out. It would be a suicide mission.

CLAUDE
You've been right all along, Suzanne. We do need to do something big. But we need to do it *right*. You keep dreaming of the flag. I keep dreaming of being attacked on the street and the stench of their bodies as they ... I am NOT going to wait until that happens to me again – or to you – God forbid (*spitting*) – and I am not going to die slowly in some labour camp or *disappear* like our friends have. I'm ready to fight. If they want me, they'll have to catch me.

SCENE 12

KALEIDOSCOPE

CLAUDE begins to transform into the Soldier with No Name. SUZANNE helps with this transformation while their dialogue is carried out in voiceovers.

CLAUDE
(*voiceover*) Autoportraiture is not a selfish, egotistical whimsy. It is practical. It is simpler to use myself rather than someone else, c'est tout.

SUZANNE
(*voiceover*) Claude was the only one I ever needed, ever wanted.

CLAUDE
(*voiceover*) I always knew. Most people know from a young age, not necessarily that they love women, or men if they're men, but they know they're different. Something sets them apart.

SUZANNE
(*voiceover, singing*) À la claire fontaine, m'en allant promener. J'ai trouvé l'eau si belle –

CLAUDE
(*voiceover*) One day they tied me to a tree and pelted me with rocks.

SUZANNE
(*voiceover, singing*) – que je m'y suis baignée –

CLAUDE
(*voiceover*) Then they left me on the road.

SUZANNE
(*voiceover*) Heil Claude Cahun! Heil Marcel Moore! Heil les gaies Parisiennes!

CLAUDE

(*voiceover*) For me, it's like my body never matched me.

SUZANNE

(*voiceover*) I had another of those dreams last night.

CLAUDE

(*voiceover*) The inside of my head was on fire when I acted like a good little girl.

SUZANNE

(*voiceover*) It was Claude's God I wanted to know.

CLAUDE

(*voiceover*) It was just us. Suzanne and me. C'est tout.

SUZANNE

(*voiceover, singing*) Jamais je ne t'oublierai.

CLAUDE

(*voiceover*) It was always just the two of us.

Dialogue is resumed by the actors. CLAUDE now wears the repurposed, German-looking army uniform that SUZANNE has mended; it had been on the mannequin.

CLAUDE

And once I've switched the flag, what's the plan? What do I need to do?

SUZANNE

It's simple: end the war, my love.

CLAUDE

And if it doesn't work? And I get captured?

SUZANNE

Then I burn all the evidence.

CLAUDE
And if they kill me?

SUZANNE
Then I take the pills. And we meet each other again on the other side.

Pause.

SUZANNE
Bonne chance, mon amour.

CLAUDE
Je t'aime, ma chère.

The sound and music build to sounds of chaos: boots on cobblestones, marching, "Heil Hitlers!" and then running, gunshots, yelling in German, gunfire. Simultaneously, CLAUDE and SUZANNE are stopped.

BANDLEADER
(*voiceover*) HALT! Halt gleich da! Sie sind festgenommen!

CLAUDE and **SUZANNE**
Took you long enough.

The sound of prison doors being slammed shut.

SCENE 13
THE CONFESSION

In a German prison on Jersey. SUZANNE and CLAUDE are held in separate cells. CLAUDE is being interrogated. SUZANNE strains to hear from her cell.

CLAUDE

What else can I tell you? It's not my problem that you don't believe me. We did it all, *for years*. All by our lonesome. Without any man. And I know Suzanne has been telling you the same thing! It's you and your people who are ignoring the facts! We're not covering for anyone. We didn't have a leader. No man at the helm. No Mr. X. It was just us: the slogans, the leaflets, the propaganda.

As for the switched flag at the very heart of your precious HQ – that was me. Alone. That was way too easy, by the way: I had the French flag rolled up in my trousers. No one doubted me for a second. I can't believe how blind you can be. I walked all the way through the town to the barracks, all the way inside your headquarters, and executed each part of the plan. Leaflets in your officers' coat pockets, check. Revolver stolen and placed in *my* pocket, check. Radio in the mess hall switched from Radio Berlin to the BBC, check. Portrait of your Führer defaced, check. Requisite "Heil Hitlers" and heel-clicking, check. Did you know I made it all the way to your Kommandant's office and tasted some of his whisky? It was lovely.

His secretary is pretty good-looking, wouldn't you say? ... For all your worries about a gang of resisters storming the barracks, your security is shit. The only reason you caught me is because I drank too much of that whisky and made a pass at your Kommandant's secretary ... I was out of practice, as was my German ... hélas. That wasn't part of the plan. But what did I have to lose? I was as good as dead anyway. Vive la France! Long live the King!

(*singing*) Allons enfants de la Patrie!

Le jour de gloire est arrivé!

CLAUDE reels back from being slapped.

SUZANNE takes up the song and bangs on a bucket; the BANDLEADER and other defiant voices join from the prison to sing "La Marseillaise."

SUZANNE and the BANDLEADER
(*singing with recorded voices from all around the prison, rough, rowdy, a cappella*) Contre nous de la tyrannie,

L'étendard sanglant est levé;

L'étendard sanglant est levé.

CLAUDE
You hear that?! (*shouting*) I hear you, Suzanne! Vive la France!

ALL
(*singing*) Aux armes, citoyens!

Formez vos bataillons!

CLAUDE is hit again.

ALL
(*singing, but getting less coherent*) Marchons, marchons!

Qu'un sang impur

Abreuve nos sillons!

CLAUDE is hit again. SUZANNE is hit. The singing stops abruptly.

CLAUDE

Fuck you. I'm not lying! There is no Mr. X! Oh my God, what kind of proof do you need? I executed the plan at your HQ – not Suzanne – she had nothing to do with that – but somehow you can't get it through your skulls that anyone other than a man could do anything against you. I'm sorry your little boy soldiers were so scared of ... two old ... *spinsters* ... But I can't confess to something that isn't true. It was just us. Suzanne and me. C'est tout. (*to the audience*) It was always just the two of us. But believe what you like. We know what we did.

SCENE 14
LIBÉRATION

Marching, victorious music of liberation and triumph. "La Marseillaise" reprise.

CLAUDE and SUZANNE reunite after the Liberation.

RADIO
(*voiceover*) This is the BBC World Service bringing you Prime Minister Winston Churchill: Hostilities will end officially at one minute after midnight tonight, Tuesday the 8th of May, 1945. But in the interests of saving lives, the "ceasefire" began yesterday to be sounded along all the fronts. And our dear Channel Islands are also to be freed today. The German war is therefore at an end. Today is Victory in Europe Day. The war is over! I repeat: the war is over! The Germans are retreating. Paris has been liberated! Belgium is free. The Dutch are still starving. That fucker Hitler is dead. The Americans are taking credit for everything, but they will have the horrific task of liberating the camps and won't ever forget it –

SCENE 15

AN ODE TO THE LIBERATION

CLAUDE
May we present ...

CLAUDE and SUZANNE
An Ode to the Liberation.

SUZANNE
By Claude and Marcel //

CLAUDE
By Marcel and Claude //

CLAUDE
(*to the BANDLEADER*) Maestro, some music if you please ...

Musical flourish.

SUZANNE
Two men at the bistro:

CLAUDE
Hé ho, camarade?

SUZANNE
Oui, mon homme?

CLAUDE
Are we still in prison?

SUZANNE
Non, mon ami. We are at the bistro in the village. The war is over.

CLAUDE
Does this mean we can eat cheese again?

SUZANNE
Oui, mon ami.

CLAUDE
Vive la France.

SUZANNE
Long live the King.

CLAUDE
Hé ho, camarade?

SUZANNE
Oui, mon gros?

CLAUDE
If the war is over, does that mean we are free?

Musical flourish.

CLAUDE
Two men meet on the road:

SUZANNE
Bonjour, Pierre.

CLAUDE
Bonjour, Jean.

SUZANNE
I wonder if you could tell me – has Madame Lévi come home?

CLAUDE
Yes, she came back just a few days ago ... but not
Monsieur Lévi ...

SUZANNE
Aaah ... quelle dommage.

CLAUDE

Hélas ... and have you seen Mademoiselle Schwob and Mademoiselle Malherbe since they were freed?

SUZANNE

Non, not yet. How long were they imprisoned for, in the end? A year?

CLAUDE

Ah, I don't remember. How long were those fuckers here?

SUZANNE

I don't remember. Forever? Ten years?

CLAUDE

Five years. Five years that felt like ten years.

SUZANNE

You got old in that time, mon ami.

CLAUDE

You died in that time, mon gros.

Musical flourish.

SUZANNE

Two men at the bistro, bis:

CLAUDE

Hé ho, camarade?

SUZANNE

Oui, mon homme?

CLAUDE

Are we still in prison?

SUZANNE

Non! We are again at the bistro in the village!

CLAUDE

Oh. D'accord ... hé ho, camarade? When we were in prison, did anything funny happen?

SUZANNE

Funny?! (*beat*) Well, there was that one time someone tried to hang himself, but he couldn't get his pyjamas to knot together quite right and it was awkward and eventually he cried out "au secours!" until one of the guards came in and untied him. That was pretty funny, because he did not die.

CLAUDE

Ha ha! Oh yeah! And I remember when one of those two old ladies tried to kill herself and couldn't! I can't remember if it was Mademoiselle Malherbe or Mademoiselle Schwob. But *anyway*, she tried to cut up her wrists but the knife she had stolen wasn't sharp enough and she was bleeding and she was crying, and then the other lady, she was in a different cell and she couldn't help her, but she could hear her crying, and then *she* was crying, and it was terrible.

SUZANNE

Nom de Dieu! Mon homme! That wasn't funny at all.

CLAUDE

Non?

SUZANNE

Non! That wasn't funny at all!

Musical flourish.

CLAUDE

In the market:

SUZANNE

Bonjour, Michelle.

CLAUDE

Bonjour, Sylvie. Did you hear what I heard about how our two lady artists survived their captivity?

SUZANNE

Yes! I did! They had sex with the guards!

CLAUDE

Mon Dieu, non! (*tittering*) How crude! No, it was because the officers needed permission from Hitler himself to execute female prisoners ... and somehow their execution kept getting delayed and delayed until finally Jersey was liberated!

SUZANNE

But they could have been killed!

CLAUDE

They *should* have been killed. (*beat*) They're Jews! (*beat*) But they weren't killed, they survived.

SUZANNE

Not everyone survived.

CLAUDE

No. Not everyone survived.

Final musical flourish.

SUZANNE and CLAUDE take their bows. CLAUDE disappears. SUZANNE is alone.

SCENE 16

FEBRUARY 19, 1972

At the top of the scene, SUZANNE is at the trunk, as in the prologue, with a notebook.

SUZANNE

My love. I've been reading through all our old papers. At least what remained after the Germans raided the house while we were in prison. I found the manuscript to the "Tell-All Memoir" Adrienne had asked you to write all those years ago. You never told me you had taken up her challenge – it's beautiful.

I liked reading about us when we were young, and about you, in your voice. I wish I had known you were working on it. I would have encouraged you: it's not *at all* a second-rate book written by and for old ladies! I wish you could have finished this memoir ... I've been amusing myself by writing some responses, adding a few confessions of my own to complement yours. I made it a two-hander! A duet. Like our old theatricals.

I'm *tired*. I went to the doctor last week, and he says I'm as healthy as a horse – he said I could live for decades. Can you believe it? Decades! I asked if he could prescribe a quick cancer like the one that did in Gertrude, but he didn't think that was funny. I still feel guilty that you died when you did. You should have lived until a hundred and twenty. I know it was our time in prison that weakened you, and you never blamed me for what got us there – you just blamed those bastards – but you were never the same again.

After you died, my pictures were full of your ghost ...

I'm going to make sure that you're remembered correctly, so I've burned everything I could find that suggests I helped you with the autoportraits – some of your notes, my memoirs. The autoportraits are yours now, entirely. I used to care, but I don't care now. More than anything, I want you to be remembered for your boldness, your inventiveness, your courage, your brilliance. The autoportraits can do that. My final work is this: to make sure you're going to be remembered as you wanted to be, and it makes me glad ... my Claude. L.S.M.

Elles s'aiment. Now for one last Kaddish in your name, my love.

> *SUZANNE places a stone as if on a gravestone. She lights a candle and whispers a prayer as she gathers up several stones and puts them into her pockets.*

À bientôt, mon amour.

EPILOGUE

SUZANNE walks towards the shore. There is CLAUDE in the water, waving like in the Act 1 prologue, or simply listening or waiting after the previous monologue: CLAUDE has heard all of Suzanne's words. Now CLAUDE beckons for SUZANNE to join them. This time SUZANNE walks towards CLAUDE. They take hands and hold on.

Projection or video of two images, Suzanne Malherbe / Marcel Moore looking into mirror, *and* Self portrait (reflected in mirror), *merge with photos of the two actors recreating the same photographs.*

The theatre lights dim with the rush of the seascape until the only light is the flame of the remembrance candle.

—FIN—

Claude Cahun (1894–1954), *Self portrait (reflected in mirror)*, 1928, courtesy of the Jersey Heritage Collections

Claude Cahun (1894–1954), *Suzanne Malherbe / Marcel Moore looking into mirror*, 1928, courtesy of the Jersey Heritage Collections

ACKNOWLEDGMENTS

The writing, development, and production of this play would not have been possible without the financial and professional support of the Canada Council for the Arts; the City of Ottawa Cultural Funding program; the Ontario Arts Council (OAC) Recommender Grants for Theatre Creators program, which provided writing grants from the Shaw Festival, the Ottawa Fringe Festival, and Cabaret Theatre; the OAC Playwright in Residence program; Great Canadian Theatre Company (GCTC); the National Arts Centre (NAC); TACTICS; and undercurrents festival. The publication of this play, a dream come true, is thanks to the enthusiasm and dedication of the team at Talonbooks.

I have enormous appreciation for Lora Krasteva, Robin Skyer, and Zhui Ning Chang, the founders of the UK's Global Voices Theatre, who presented a staged excerpt from *Heartlines* as part of their event Global Jewish Voices. Their enthusiasm brought forth a podcast series hosted by Victor Esses and a beautiful anthology entitled *Global Jewish Plays: Five Works by Jewish Playwrights from around the World.*

I would like to thank editors Evan Tsitsias and Bilal Baig for including Claude's monologue "Outsider" in their urgent collection of essays, monologues, and scenes *This is Beyond: A Time Capsule of Queer Experience.*

I would also like to acknowledge the following people who offered practical help with the writing, development, and production of *Heartlines*: Lawrence Aronovitch, Rebecca Benson, Liz Bolton, Rebecca Eamon Campbell, Eric Coates, Eleanor Crowder, Dominique Gais, Patrick Gauthier, Dr. Michelle Gewurtz, Scottie Irving, Brittney Johnston, Jillian Keiley, Sarah Kitz, Nathan Medd, Hugh Neilson, Emily Pearlman, Ludmylla Reis, Laurie Shannon, Sarah Garton Stanley, Andrea Steinwand, Bronwyn Steinberg, David Waisvisz, Jacques Waisvisz, and Martine Waisvisz.

Finally, I would like to acknowledge the extraordinary insights offered by performers Maryse Fernandes and Margo MacDonald, who developed the characters of Suzanne and Claude and gave more life to them than I alone could have.

LIST OF ARTWORKS

Scenes in *Heartlines* refer to the following works of art by Claude Cahun and Marcel Moore.

ACT 1

Prologue: Claude Cahun, *Autoportrait*, ca. 1927 (I Am In Training Don't Kiss Me)
Scene 2: Claude Cahun, *Untitled (duogram)*, ca. 1919 or 1929
Scene 5: Claude Cahun, *Autoportrait*, 1927 (Claude with aviator goggles and scarf), or other self-portrait
Scene 6: Claude Cahun, *Aveux non avenus* series, ca. 1929
Scene 7: Claude Cahun, *Autoportrait*, ca. 1928 (Claude with shaved head and sleeveless shirt)

ACT 2

Scene 5: Claude Cahun, *Autoportrait*, ca. 1929–1930 (two figures lying parallel, head to toe)
Scenes 6, 7, 8, and 9: Marcel Moore's propaganda cartoons
Scene 10: Claude Cahun, *Combat de pierres*, 1931
Scene 16: Claude Cahun, autoportraits and negatives of Claude Cahun in the garden and at the seaside in Jersey, ca. 1948
Epilogue: Claude Cahun, *Suzanne Malherbe/Marcel Moore looking into mirror*, 1928, and *Self portrait (reflected in mirror)*, 1928

NOTES ON MUSIC

The *Heartlines* professional premiere included music and a soundscape composed by Scottie Irving. Playing live onstage as the Bandleader, he performed on seven instruments: harp, piano, snare drum, synthesizer, melodica, accordion, and voice. Here is an edited version of his notes.

ACT 1

Prologue: Seascape with harp improvisation on "À la claire fontaine."
Scene 1: Piano improvisation on the "À la claire fontaine" theme.
Scene 2: Tacet.
Scene 3: Claude's text underscored by ostinato-based improvisation on piano with swells on accordion drone. Minor key. Suzanne's text underscored by seascape with delicate treble piano improvisation, accompanied by sustained accordion chords. Major key.
Scene 4: Travelling music on accordion. After the concluding flourish and before "Paris – la ville lumière," accordion music continues "Parisian-cliché style."
Scene 5: Harp improvisation for Claude, piano improvisation for Suzanne.
Scene 6: Stormy piano introduction for Claude's entrance. Then tacet until the end of the scene, when a waltz begins again to accompany their dancing.
Scene change: Brisk and gavotte-like music on accordion.
Scene 7: Begin in silence. Understated music with very gradual development; drum, piano figures, and accordion swells mirror the sexual tension on stage. Similar to Ravel's *Boléro* in length and gradualism, but with a militaristic march for a climax of intensity. By the middle and end of the scene, the music is quite threatening, and by the end of the scene, the music has reached a "local" climax, although the ultimate musical climax must be saved for the end of Act 1.
Scene 8: Snare drum evokes military marching, and brusque, rhythmic accordion chords and improvised treble figures underscore the news broadcast in a manner reminiscent of Holst's "Mars, the Bringer of War," from *The Planets*.

ACT 2

Prologue: Bombastic snare fanfare re-introduces the music from the end of Act 1.

Scene 1: Seascape. Gentle ostinato-based piano improvisation with Lydian mode feel. Gradual development.

Scene 2: For odes, lively oompah piano improvisation, darkly absurd, each vignette concluding with a musical flourish, as in all the odes. A clear cadence concludes each vignette.

Scene 3: Dissonant legato waltz, nocturne-style, as if Satie's "Gymnopédie No. 1" were set in extended tonality.

Scene 4: Subliminal electric hum when lights are on; silence when they are off.

Scene 5: Piano, cold and staccato, brittle and dissonant, mimicking Claude's utterances.

Scene 6: Slow military beat on drum, as if a soldier were passing by, at the start and end of the scene. Tacet for the rest.

Scene 7: Rain falling. Subliminal electric hum. Snare drum. The sound of a drip or leaking or ticking hints at upcoming adventure music in the "Paper Route" scene.

Scene 8: A few bars of military beat open the scene. Clock ticking and rain leaking sounds are louder now.

Scene 9: A modern drum loop underscores the action cinematically, à la *Mission: Impossible*. Furtive Morse code figures on Rhodes piano are by turns humorous and tense.

Scene 10: Electric hum. Piano provides low-register rumbles and crisp, high-register dyads. Synthesizer provides blade-like reverse cymbal effect mirroring Claude's pain. The scene culminates with high-pitched wail on melodica. Military drum concludes the scene.

Scene 11: Electric hum rises and falls in intensity. The wail from the previous scene is reprised on melodica during Claude's brief flashback.

Scene 12: Prerecorded collage soundscape of Claude and Suzanne's voices speaking previously heard lines and singing "À la claire fontaine." Disorienting, with reverb. Live improvised rumbles, swells, and runs on piano, drum, and harp. At "And once I've switched the flag," sound diminishes but must not disappear. At "Je t'aime, ma chère," comes the ultimate climax. The sound and music erupt into chaos: boots on cobblestones, marching, and "Heil Hitlers!"

followed by sounds of running, gunshots, airplanes, yelling in German, and gunfire. Even more intense live improvised rumbles, swells, and runs on piano, drum, and harp.

Scene 13: Snare drum used to signify punches, hits, and slaps.

Scene 14: Music of liberation and triumph. "La Marseillaise" in a broad setting on accordion.

Scene 15: The clown scenes are underscored by improvised klezmeresque oom-pah accordion music, prestissimo as a runaway train. The mood is irreverent. As in Act 1, Scene 2, a clear cadence concludes each vignette before the next key in the progression.

Scene 16: Seascape with harp improvisation on "À la claire fontaine."

Epilogue: Sound and music continue as in the previous scene.

Sarah Gabriella Waisvisz is a playwright, director, and performer. Her multidisciplinary solo show *Monstrous*, about being of mixed Afro-Caribbean and Jewish roots, was published in *Alt.theatre* 13.3 and was performed across Canada and the United States. She has been Playwright in Residence at Great Canadian Theatre Company and at the National Arts Centre, and she directed Donna-Michelle St. Bernard's film *Witness Shift* for Obsidian Theatre / CBC Arts' filmed anthology *21 Black Futures*. Sarah is an assistant professor at the Dan School of Drama and Music at Queen's University.

Photo: Gary Stein